MW00993718

"For what doth it profit a man if a gift is bestowed upon him, and he receive not the gift? Behold, he rejoices not in that which is given unto him, neither rejoices in him who is the giver of the gift."

Doctrine & Covenants 88:33

"When the morning stars sang together,
and all the sons of God shouted for joy"

Job 38:7

His Gift

by Richard Paul Evans and Tracy Michele Evans
Illustrated by Anne Marie Oborn

ARCADIA
Publishing

Thank you, Tracy, for creating such a beautiful theme. Thank you, Anne, for dressing this story in adornment worthy of the message. Most of all I acknowledge Him—the giver of many gifts and boundless love.

— R.P.E.

Special thanks to my husband, Scott, for supporting, loving and putting all the pieces together; and to my brother-in-law, Richard, for his ever-present vision and talent. I am especially grateful for the hands and spirit of Anne Marie Oborn, which together have created something beautiful; and Cynthia Dye for her wonderful support, assistance and talent. I must also thank Paul Shiramizu, who has been an invaluable part of this team. And my friend, Cindy B., for her encouragement. Greatest thanks, however, must be given to the giver of all gifts.

— T.M.E.

Thanks to Scott, Tracy, Rick, and Cynthia Dye for their help with my artwork.

— A.M.O.

His Gift

Text Copyright © 2001 by Richard Paul Evans and Tracy Michele Evans

Illustration Copyright © 2001 by Anne Marie Oborn

All rights reserved. No part of this book may be reproduced in any form or by any means without permission from the publisher, Arcadia Publishing. The views expressed herein are the responsibility of the authors and do not necessarily represent the position of Arcadia Publishing.

Published By Arcadia Publishing
805 West 1700 South
Salt Lake City, Utah 84104

Cover Design and page layout by Paul Shiramizu, Graphic Design

Photographic Assistance, Cynthia Dye

ISBN 1-930817-11-8

Library of Congress Control Number: 2001012345

Printed in The United States of America

2 3 4 5 6 7 8 9 10

To Abigail (my little Chester).

– R.P.E.

To my husband, Scott, and my children,
Paul, Michelle, Shaun, Spencer and Tyler.
My beautiful gifts.

– T.M.E.

To my husband Garth and the future generations of
Oborns, Gruwells, Burtons and to Rachel "Our Little Scrap of Heaven."

– A.M.O.

One gentle spring day, when I was a child, my mother and I went for a walk in the garden behind our house. She took me in her arms and told me a story.

"A long time ago," she said, "far away in a land above the clouds, lived a large family of children. It was a beautiful land without worry or care. These were happy children, for they had almost everything they desired. But not all. More than anything else they wanted to be like their Father."

Their Father was a marvelous father. He could make wonders, from great, majestic mountains to small, beautiful butterflies. Though the children marveled at all His creations, their Father told them that *they* were His greatest creation. Moreover, their Father knew all things. He knew why the wind blew and why the grass was green.

But what He knew best was how to love each of His children. His greatest desire, Father often told them, was to see *them* happy."

One day Father called for His children. The children ran to Him, for they loved to be with Father. They gathered where they always did—at the large meadow where the grass was brightest and softest. It was the children's favorite place in that land, for Father had made it especially for them. There were flowers of colors more brilliant than even a child could imagine and trees that stretched so high their tops could not be seen."

Today,' Father said in a voice as beautiful as music, yet as mighty as a great river, 'I shall tell you of the gift I have prepared for you.' Father had given His children many great gifts. He had even made for them a place called *earth* where they would someday go to learn to be more like Him. But He spoke of this new gift with a reverence that filled the children with excitement. Even the flowers and trees seemed to bend with anticipation."

Gently lifting a child to His knee, He said, 'I know your hearts' greatest wish, and it pleases me that you wish to be like me. For this cause I have made a gift for each one of you.'"

This gift is different from the others I have given you,' Father explained, 'for this gift you may take with you when you leave my presence and go to live on earth.'"

This gift is a body like mine,' Father said. At this the children shouted with joy, for this was the thing they desired most. Father smiled. He explained that this body was a special place where their spirits would dwell when they left the heavens and went to live in their new home on earth. 'I have prepared this gift in my own image that you may remember whose child you are.' This made the children very happy, for they had been taught that they would not be able to remember all of Father's gifts, or even Father, when they left His presence."

Like your spirit, your body is divine,' Father said, 'for it too was created from my love for you. Your body is as unique as the snowflakes I have made. Every one of them is different, yet each is beautiful in its own way.'"

This body will bring you great joy. If used correctly, your body will help keep your spirit pure and holy. You must be careful with this gift, for it is fragile and of great worth. You must always protect it, for you will be given only one. There will be those who will give your body things to hurt and enslave it,' Father warned. 'These things will harm your spirit as well.'"

You will honor me,' Father said, 'by honoring the gift which I have made for you. You will show me your love by how you care for my gift.' All of the children wanted to honor Father for they loved Him very much. 'If you will do as I have instructed,' Father said, 'one day you shall return home to me. Then I shall greet you at this very meadow.'"

When my mother finished telling me this story she smiled and held me close. "You will know it is Him," my mother whispered, "because you will look like Him and He will look like you. Then He will hold you like this, and you will feel His love, and He will call you His Child."

$\mathcal{A}$nd it will feel like home."

WHAT IS THE MOST IMPORTANT THING
WE CAN DO FOR OUR AT-RISK CHILDREN?

In 1996, Richard and Keri Evans sponsored a childrens' welfare conference to discuss this question. The answer was to create The Christmas Box House International, an organization dedicated to helping abused and neglected children by building special shelter/assessment facilities. The Christmas Box House is a one-stop shelter and assessment facility for abused and neglected children—children who are currently shuffled from agency to agency, from police officer to doctor to caseworker, before being thrust into a new home. At The Christmas Box House all these visits occur on-site, providing familiarity and comfort at a difficult time. In addition, The Christmas Box House brings together child advocates, including foster families, Children's Advocacy centers, the Centers for Children's Justice, and government agencies, to provide and enhance services for at-risk children.

For more information about The Christmas Box House, or to make a contribution, please visit our web site at

www.richardpaulevans.com

or write us at

Richard Paul Evans
P.O. Box 1416
Salt Lake City, Utah 84110